Bert's New Collection

A Story About What Belongs Together

Bert's New Collection

A Story About What Belongs Together

By Jocelyn Stevenson
Illustrated by Marsha Winborn

On Sesame Street, Luis is performed by Emilio Delgado, and Maria
is performed by Sonia Manzano.

Featuring Jim Henson's
Sesame Street Muppets

A Sesame Street/Golden Press Book
Published by Western Publishing Company, Inc.,
in conjunction with Children's Television Workshop.

Bert sat on the floor in the middle of all his treasures: his bottle caps, his paper clips, his rulers, his argyle socks, his sponges, his hats with feathers, and his pink erasers. He sang a little song:

"Collecting rulers is groovy,
Collecting sponges is mellow.
Erasers, paper clips, bottle caps, too!
Oh, I'm such a happy fellow!"

Bert remembered how he started collecting things.

When Little Bert discovered sponges, he began gathering all different kinds. He took his entire collection into the tub whenever he took a bath.

When Luis taught Little Bert how to measure, Bert began to find and keep rulers of all lengths.

When Herry Monster opened a bottle of something for Little Bert to drink, he asked, "What's that, Herry?"

"It's Figgy Fizz," said Herry.

"No, I mean the wonderful thing you took off the top of the bottle," said Little Bert. And that was the beginning of Bert's lifelong love of bottle caps.

A little while later Betty Lou walked in. "Hi, Bert!" she said. "Boy, look at all those great things you've collected." Betty Lou walked around Bert and admired everything. "I wish I knew how to collect things," she said.

"First you have to think of something really neat to collect, like envelopes or rubber bands or pictures of sheep," said Bert.

Betty Lou shook her head.

"I know...pencils!" Bert had always wanted to collect pencils.

"No, not for me, Bert," Betty Lou said.

Bert thought for a moment. "Sometimes the best
place to start is your pockets. That's where I found my
very first pink eraser."

Betty Lou looked in her jacket pockets. Nothing in
there. Then she looked in her shirt pockets. Nothing in
there, either. Finally she stuck her hand in the back
pocket of her pants and pulled out a brown button.

"All I can find is a brown button," she said.
"You found a *brown button*?" said Bert. "You
:ky duck! Brown buttons are probably *the*
:tiest things in the world to collect! Come on—
's go find lots more!"
"But, Bert, I don't want to collect brown..."
"Pay close attention," Bert interrupted. "I'll
ow you how." Bert grabbed Betty Lou's hand
d dragged her out the door.

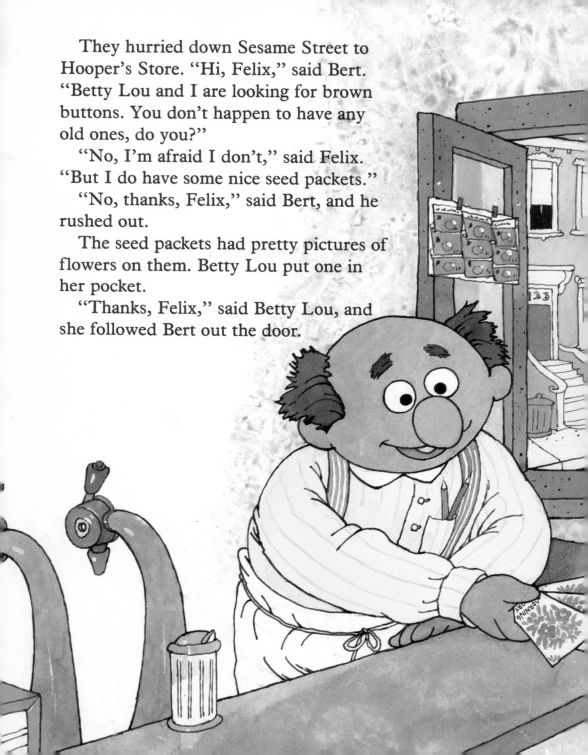

They hurried down Sesame Street to
Hooper's Store. "Hi, Felix," said Bert.
"Betty Lou and I are looking for brown
buttons. You don't happen to have any
old ones, do you?"

"No, I'm afraid I don't," said Felix.
"But I do have some nice seed packets."

"No, thanks, Felix," said Bert, and he
rushed out.

The seed packets had pretty pictures of
flowers on them. Betty Lou put one in
her pocket.

"Thanks, Felix," said Betty Lou, and
she followed Bert out the door.

"We'll ask Big Bird next," Bert said.

Big Bird was reading a book. "Hi, Big Bird!" said Bert. "Do you have any brown buttons for our collection?"

"Sorry, Bert," said Big Bird. "I'm all out of buttons, but I have a pretty piece of yarn."

"No, thanks," said Bert.

Betty Lou put the yarn in her pocket.

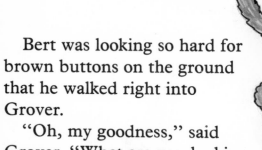

Bert was looking so hard for brown buttons on the ground that he walked right into Grover.

"Oh, my goodness," said Grover. "What are you looking for? Have you lost your quarter to call your mommy?"

"No, Grover," said Bert. "We are looking for brown buttons! Do you have one that you could spare?"

Grover looked at his arms. He looked at his legs. He looked at his tummy. He looked at himself all over. "Oh, I am so sorry," he said. "I do not seem to have a single brown button. seem to have only blue fur.

"Wait a minute!" cried Grover. He opened his paper sack. "In this little bag I am carrying some cute little patches that my mommy gave me. Would you like one?"

Bert sighed. "We're not collecting patches, Grover."

But Betty Lou took a patch and put it in her pocket.

"Well, Betty Lou," said Bert, "I guess we'll have to look in my very own private collecting places. First—the cracks in the sidewalk."

They peered into the cracks in the sidewalk. There were no brown buttons, but Betty Lou found some string. She put it into her pocket.

"Now we'll look around the bicycle racks," said Bert. They found no brown buttons, but Betty Lou picked up a paper wrapper.

"This is terrible," moaned Bert. "Let's try my last secret place—under the picnic table in the park."

There were no buttons under the table, but Betty Lou found a marble and some shiny stones.

"Come on, Betty Lou," said Bert, "we're not going to find anything here."

Then, just as Bert was getting up...

"A brown button!" he cried. "I see one!"
He grabbed at it.

The brown button was attached to Maria's coat.

"Bert, what are you doing?" gasped Maria.

"Collecting brown buttons," said Bert, scrambling to his feet.

"Well, I'm sorry. You can't have the button from my coat," Maria said. "But you can have the stamps on my letter from Puerto Rico."

"No, thanks, Maria," said Bert sadly. "We're not collecting stamps. I'll give you one of my best paper clips for that button instead. How about it, Maria, huh? A fair trade, huh?"

Maria shook her head. "A paper clip just won't fasten my coat, Bert."

Betty Lou put the stamps in her pocket.

"I give up, Betty Lou," said Bert. "Let's go home."

"Okay," said Betty Lou. "My pockets are full anyway."

On the way to 123 Sesame Street, Bert and Betty Lou ran into Farley, who was flipping his baseball cards.

Bert could not resist. "Farley," he said, "would you happen to have any brown buttons for a collection?"

"No," answered Farley, "but I have a double of Homer Hadley that you can have."

"We're collecting brown buttons, not baseball cards," said Bert.

But Betty Lou took the card.

"Well, Betty Lou," Bert said when they got home, "I told you collecting isn't easy. I guess you're just not cut out for it."

But Betty Lou was busy emptying her pockets. She carefully laid out the things she'd gotten that day.

Betty Lou set out...

a seed packet

a piece of yarn

a patch

string

a marble

a paper wrapper

two shiny stones

stamps

HOMER HADLEY

#3

a Homer Hadley baseball card

"Look, Betty Lou! Everything you collected today is BLUE!" said Bert.

"Right, Bert," said Betty Lou. "This is my blue collection."

"Hey, that's really keen!" he said. "Congratulations, Betty Lou. That's the very best blue collection I've ever seen!"

"Thank you, Bert. And because you taught me how to collect things, I want to give you something."

Betty Lou reached into her pocket and pulled out the first thing she had found. "Here, Bert. This is the first brown button for your new collection!"